Life of a Wolf   Age 5 to 8

Growing Up Wild
WOLVES

Sandra Markle

Atheneum Books for Young Readers
NEW YORK · LONDON · TORONTO · SYDNEY · SINGAPORE

This is a gray wolf just being born! At birth, each pup was encased in a tough sac. Mom broke the sac with her teeth and licked it away. Look how small and helpless the pups are. Their eyes are sealed shut and will stay that way for about two weeks. They can't hear yet, and they don't have any teeth. The pups also can't produce enough heat to keep themselves warm. They'll need to stay close to Mom's warm body for about three weeks.

Snug in the family's rock den, the wolf pups sleep curled up in Mom's thick fur. Four or five times a day hunger will wake them. Then they'll follow their noses and the scent of milk to find Mom's nipples. When the pups finish nursing and are dozing again, Mom licks their tummies to get them to pass wastes. Then she quickly licks these up. That keeps the den clean so no smells will attract a hungry enemy like a mountain lion or a bear.

Three weeks of nursing and growing change the wolf pups. Their eyes are open but at first they are blue. They won't turn amber yellow until the pups are older. Their ears stand up instead of lying limp, but they're still round, not pointed, the way they will be later. Their noses are short and fuzzy too. In fact, the pups are so compact they look like furry balls.

The pups sleep less now. Besides Mom's milk, they sometimes get a scrap of meat, a stick, or a piece of hide to chew with their new baby teeth. When they're awake, the pups are bursting with energy. They wrestle with each other and climb over Mom. They also explore the den. It isn't long before the pups find their way to the den opening.

Imagine discovering the world for the first time! The pups are curious but easily frightened. A puff of wind is enough to send them scurrying back inside.

Day by day, the pups' natural curiosity coaxes them a little farther away from the den. The world is full of new sights and sounds. But it's the new smells that are the most powerful lure. Smell is a wolf's best sense—as much as a hundred times more sensitive than yours!

When this pup suddenly finds himself alone and out of sight of the den, he howls. But since a pup's vocal cords are not yet fully developed, the only sound that comes out is "yup-yup."

Still it's enough to bring Mom to the rescue. Her bite is powerful enough to break a prey's bones, but she grabs her pup gently. Her sharp teeth don't even break his skin as she carries him back to the den.

The pups no longer need Mom's constant attention, so she can again go hunting with the pack. That's important to the whole pack because she is one of the best hunters. Usually only the most dominant male and female in the pack mate each year and have pups. Then the whole pack helps raise the young, guarding them, bringing them food, and playing with them. So when Mom goes hunting, at least one member of the pack may stay behind to pup-sit.

As one of the pack leaders, Mom gets to eat first, so she gets some of the most nourishing parts. She rips off meat and fat, gulping it down. Then she quickly heads back to her pups. Her digestive system goes to work at once to break down this food.

By the time she reaches the pups, she has more than milk for them. The pups eagerly lick Mom's mouth. This triggers her to throw up some of her partly digested meal. The pups gulp this down. Then they rush up to other members of the pack to beg for more food.

Still hungry, this pup nurses too. Wolf pups continue to nurse until they're about nine weeks old.

Growing Up Wild
WOLVES

Other Books by Sandra Markle

Growing Up Wild: Bears

Outside and Inside Alligators
Outside and Inside Bats
Outside and Inside Birds
Outside and Inside Dinosaurs
Outside and Inside Kangaroos
Outside and Inside Sharks
Outside and Inside Snakes
Outside and Inside Spiders

Pioneering Frozen Worlds
Pioneering Ocean Depths

Discovering Graph Secrets
Math Mini-Mysteries
Measuring Up
Science to the Rescue

Also

Gone Forever Illustrated by Felipe Dávalos

When the pups are about six weeks old, the pack leaves the den site. Some packs move from spot to spot as the pups continue to grow. Others move just once to a meeting site—a place where the pack can get together between hunts to feed the pups. If the pack catches a really large caribou or a musk ox, adults will stay near the kill to feed for several days. Then one of the adults may lead the pups to the kill to share the food.

Wolf pups have toys. This time it's a piece of fur from the kill. The pups sink their baby teeth into the tasty, soft skin. They tug and tug until their pretend prey rips apart. Another time, one of the adults may bring the pups a bone or even a small dead animal like a rabbit— a taste of what they'll one day be hunting.

Soon the young hunters-in-training are on the trail of prey of their own. At first, this little pack only chases bugs or rodents, like mice. Sometimes they catch their prey and are rewarded with a tasty mouthful. Other times, the prey escapes.

Always curious and hungry, this wolf pup is finding out if a leaf is tasty. See its small baby teeth?

These wolf pups are playing, but they're also learning an important wolf skill—how to show who's dominant or in charge. In each pack there may be several levels of dominance—adults over pups and stronger adults over weaker ones. Dominance may be shown with just a stare. But usually, the stronger wolf stands over the weaker one.

Playing is hard work, so the pups take frequent naps.

By the time the pups are about two months old, they've changed a lot. Their ears are pointed and able to turn to help pick up sounds. Their legs are longer to prepare them for long runs through tall grass and snow. Their noses are longer too, and their sense of smell is even better developed. A wolf can smell a prey animal from as far away as a few miles if the wind is blowing in its direction.

Even the pups' hair is changing. Instead of puppy fuzz, they're growing their adult coat. It has a layer of underhair to trap body heat. Over this is the longer coat of guard hairs. Their muzzle has sensory hairs to help them feel their way through tight places when it's dark.

Look at these sixteen-week-old pups running with the pack. Wolves can run as fast as 64 kilometers (40 miles) per hour. Like the adults, their feet have developed thick toes that can be held together for speed or spread apart for better traction.

The pups are also cutting their adult teeth. They'll soon have a powerful mouth full of forty-two sharp teeth.

This young wolf is being reminded who's boss. Obeying an adult can mean staying safe during a hunt. Nearly half of all young wolves die before they're a year old. Mistakes are the main cause. Some young wolves get too close to a strong prey animal while the pack is hunting. Some get caught by an enemy, such as a grizzly bear. Others become sick and die.

This wolf is sneaking up on a deer. While wolves run down most of their food, they try to get as close as possible before the chase begins. The art of stalking is one of the many lessons young wolves have to learn while hunting alongside the adults.

Bringing down a big elk or caribou to feed the pack takes teamwork. And the pack must be successful. Each wolf needs to eat about 1.1 kilograms (2.5 pounds) of meat each day to stay healthy and be active.

The young wolves are nearly full grown by winter. They have their adult teeth. Their eyes are amber yellow, and they can produce a throaty howl. Most importantly, they've learned how to help the pack hunt. When the new pups are born in the spring, the young adults will help provide for the pack's expanding family. Then the growing-up process will begin all over again.

Glossary

CARIBOU (kâr e bü) These animals live in herds and travel with the season in order to continue grazing. Both males and females have antlers. **15, 29**

DEER (dir) They eat many different kinds of plants and plant parts, including nuts, fungi, grass, and twigs. The males develop antlers that are shed and regrown each year to compete for mates. **28**

DEN (den) A cave, a hole in the ground, or nearly any other place a female wolf can have her pups and keep them warm for about the first three weeks of their lives. **5–6, 8–9, 15**

ENEMY (e-nə-mē) A wolf's enemy is any person or animal who would try to hurt or kill it. A full-grown wolf's enemies are mainly people and bears. The smaller the wolf pup, the more enemies it has. **5, 26**

GRAY WOLF (grā wülf) They may be silver gray, but they can also be rusty red, cream, white, and black. There are gray wolves found all over the world. In the United States, they are sometimes called timber, tundra, arctic, or Rocky Mountain wolves. **4**

MILK (milk) Food produced in the body of female mammals, (animals that have hair and give birth to live young). Milk supplies food energy for their babies, so they can grow big enough to eat other food **5, 6, 13**

MUSK OX (mə sk äks) This animal has a long coat of hair to protect it from cold, wet weather. It lives in herds. When attacked by wolves, the heard huddles together, with the males facing out. **15**

NIPPLE (ni-pəl) The body part of a female that her baby sucks to get her milk. **5**

NURSE (nərs) To feed on a mother's milk. **5, 6, 13**

RODENT (rô-dənt) A group of animals, such as mice and squirrels. They are especially known for chisel-shaped front teeth that help them gnaw through even tough food. **18**

WRESTLE (re-səl) To push and pull in a struggle. Wolf pups practice showing each other who's the leader. Since it's play, the pup that leads one minute is likely to submit the next. **6**

ä as in c<u>a</u>rt	ā as in <u>a</u>pe	â as in <u>ai</u>r	ə as in b<u>a</u>nan<u>a</u>	ē as in <u>e</u>ven
ī as in b<u>i</u>te	ô as in <u>go</u>	ü as in r<u>u</u>le	u as in f<u>u</u>r	

31

For Rett and Kerry Crocker.

Thanks for being such wonderful friends.

The author would especially like to thank wolf expert Eric Gese

(Research Biologist and Assistant Professor, National Wildlife Research Center,

Department of Fisheries and Wildlife, Utah State University, Logan, Utah)

for sharing his enthusiasm and sixteen years of expertise.

Author's Note: While this book is about gray wolves, there are also red wolves and Mexican wolves living in North America. Red wolves are smaller than gray wolves and once ranged over the American southeast from Georgia and Florida west to Texas. As few as forty Mexican wolves may still be alive. There are also limited populations of wolves in other countries, including Spain, France, Italy, Finland, the Middle East, Russia, and countries in Asia.

Efforts are underway to restore both gray and red wolves to parts of their original range. This includes restoring gray wolves to Yellowstone National Park and red wolves to parts of the Southeast. Some people support this effort; others fear wolves will be a threat to other animals, including farm animals.

Photo Credits: Richard Kirchner: half-title, 4, 5, 7, 8, 18, 19, 30; Erwin and Peggy Bauer: 11, 14, 20, 23; Tom and Pat Leeson: 9, 13, 17, 21, 27; Michael Francis: 12, 24–25, 29; Bruce Montagne: 28;

Atheneum Books for Young Readers
An imprint of Simon & Schuster Children's Publishing Division
1230 Avenue of the Americas, New York, NY 10020

The text of this book is set in Berliner Grotesk.
Printed in Hong Kong
2 4 6 8 10 9 7 5 3 1

Library of Congress Cataloging-in-Publication Data
Markle, Sandra.
Growing up wild : wolves / Sandra Markle.—1st ed.   p. cm.
Summary: Text and color photographs show how
gray wolf cubs are born and grow up in the wild.
ISBN 0-689-81886-6
1 Wolves—Infancy—Juvenile literature. [1 Wolves. 2. Animals—Infancy.] I. Title.
QL737.C22+   599.773'139—dc21   99-54145

FIRST
EDITION